For Jim,
who helped me recognize the difference
between an existence and a human life;

for Brian,
who encouraged me to try to integrate
the perceptions this awareness gave me;

and for Bob,
my life partner and husband,
a constant source of support and encouragement,
who has always inspired me to reach higher.

Contents

Dancing with Death

Splitting the Circle

Marching to a New Drummer

Learning to Play in the Symphony

A TIARA FOR THE TWENTIETH CENTURY

Tiara:
A Pavane for a Soul in Peril

How exquisite the rubies of Cressida
A spark of blood upon the satin snow
How blinding Hagar's emeralds
Daggers of green fire
Ablaze upon bodices
Of ivory and ice
Inviting the pale garnet upon the throat of Jezebel
The poniard of platinum nestled in Bathsheba's ear

The sapphire of Melisande, the diamonds of Helen
Carve wounds upon white velvet
The opal and amethyst beckon
In damask and brocade the anointed woo the onyx eyes of Sheba
Court Francesca's tongue of beryl, Isolde's marble thigh
Embrace the alabaster flame upon the Stygian barge
Caress the torch of Cerberus at the gate
Cast aside Aaron's breastplate, the scroll of Solomon, a solitary pearl.

The Lunar Cycle

The Harp at Birth

Remember the woman's body is no rude vessel
To be snatched in hunger from the shelf
But an artifact chiseled with exquisite care
By a craftsman whose touch told him
The moment's not in that customary thrust
Of legs tangled in a labyrinth

But in finely tuned fingertips
That pluck from the filamentary rib
A single cry
You are the leaven
Who will knead this loaf
Into the bread of life.

The Harp of Eros

Your heart is no coarse vessel
To snatch in hunger from the shelf
But a cameo carved by a craftsman
Whose touch told him magic lies
In a finely tuned fingertip
Plucking from a filament the chord of love
That kneads a world
Into the bread of life.

Miscarriage

Thou Shalt Not Covet Thy Neighbor's Child
It must be #11 on that list
I stand in the A&P
She perches like a sparrow in her cart
One hand clutching a box of Cheerios
The other fondles half melted M&M's.

Delivery Room

My body is a canvas stretched
To catch a falling wing walker
Pulsing like a tom-tom in some obscure and distant jungle
Soon the cry will strike an opaque wall
Ricochet down the ivory corridor
It will wriggle like a serpent
Dancing in the dust
While attendants scurry like fat white mice.

A Former Passion for 3's

I used to worship them
They meant the pieces of the Eiffel Tower puzzle
Would slide together smoothly
The Mix 'n' Match sweaters and skirts
Would blend and never clash
The family quarrel over Xmas dinner
Wouldn't wait for termination
Till the reading of the will

Now I've got Kelly green shoes
Fuchsia hats
A mustard blouse
No one agrees it's their turn
To bake Thanksgiving pie and bring the rolls
Or leave the tip at Sardi's
The gears grind against
An odd assortment of 4's.

Esperanto

Your eyes beckon like the sea
Where anemones whisper of flesh
And purple fields
We tread water on a smile
Verbs are traps, you deputize
Finger tips, breakwaters for swells
Too strong to crest
At their appointed hour.

Alice and Dorothy:
Two Little Girls on a Marriage-Go-Round

Grey smudges blur the mirror in Wonderland
A midnight spin through a gin glazed glass
Keeps splintered dreams
From invading Alice's boudoir
Sucking blusher from her cheeks
Draining violet shadow from an eyelid at 4 A.M.

Dorothy swings a shovel under a lead sky
In a field of bulging silos and heaps of stray manure
Where the world sags
With the price of corn
Where hubby Henry enfolds her
Like an empty burlap bag
Where a cyclone is the savior
Who'll spin her to another wizard
With a promise of ruby slippers
And the magic of a rainbow.

Times of the Year

There are times of the year
One comes to dread
The end of the semester
When red ink bleeds
On blue books
Awaiting absentee owners

The last evening of the holiday
Husbands prepare for Monday's skirmish
Socks are sorted
Shirts are pressed
Armed with an attaché
He'll charge via telex and committee

There are times of the year
When the customary answer
Crumbles in the hand
When a tablet dissolves
At 4 A.M.
In a cracked glass.

The Woman Who Walks in the Museum

The woman who walks in the museum
Cannot address the Apollo Belvedere
They cannot exchange a casual word or two
As she passes through the alcove

Has she been on friendly terms
With genitals etched by napalm
Has she seen pus drip from the corner
Of a faded picture frame

Is she at odds with Raphael's Madonna
Whose pink nipples are raw and angry
As if that cherubic infant
Had gnawed all night in vain

Has she made more than a nod in the direction
Of Goya's firing squad
Has she held more than a casual conversation
With the headless torsos of Austerlitz
The stray limbs that litter
The beach at Gallipoli

The woman who walks in the museum
Speaks only to El Greco
She scales white walls
Steps into gilded frames
That house the Guernica
Breugel's devil
Durer's death
And their knights.

Da Vinci's Self-Portrait:
The Man and His Mona Lisa

The announcement was most matter of fact
The eyes that transfixed connoisseurs
Were a camera photographing
A familiar self
The smile dissected by critics
Was the fawn of nature
Outrunning
The wolf of flesh.

Corporate Spouse

Tonight's agenda calls for catering
She must remember to pass the cheese ball and the macadamia nuts
Before negotiations resume
She must make sure her smile is appropriately lacquered

Next week is the Christmas Party
Before you know it the Annual Picnic
Her portfolio is clearly labeled
National Secretaries Day

She must be properly arranged
In a spare seat at the business brunch
She must be coiffed and varnished
Lines memorized and delivered on cue

She's accustomed to lingering in the shadows
Of skyscrapers and attaché cases
Her echo is ex officio
She's a glass of wine gone sour.

Home on Mother's Day

It's like stumbling through the chimp's cage
In the San Diego Zoo
Every second I skid
On a stray banana peel
I mark the minutes by scratching
Some fresh ancestral sore
When the nursery tree bends
I swing from the bough.

Prognosis

Motherhood is a terminal disease
With brief periods of remission
Moments when the dancers spin
In a subdued light
Hours when no shred of memory
Survives to haunt the heart
Days when the ulcer throbs like a forlorn solo
Choreographed for islands
Where familiar invaders are embraced.

Diagnosis

I am suffering from a terminal illness
No miracle or wonder drug will cure me
I will enjoy periods of remission
Moments when this disease will
Spin in slow motion
Moments when no shred of memory
Survives to haunt my heart
Moments when motherhood is not some forlorn ballet
Choreographed on an island
To which familiar invaders long offshore
Are destined to return.

Mother and Daughter-in-Law

We're not freshly minted coins
Merely heirs to an old legacy
Not green recruits but seasoned veterans in the contest
We've fallen into that bear trap
Of gift certificates and birthday checks
In a chain of missed connections
Two parallel lines who fulfill their destiny
We fight an old guerrilla war
Reluctant combatants who make holiday sorties
Into one another's camp
We've been known to sign a Christmas truce.

Agape:
A Family Love Feast

Dearly beloved
We are gathered here
To celebrate the demise
Of yet another year
In Sonny's undistinguished
But fiscally sound career

The family stag presides
Over a plate of rusty lettuce
A mildly deranged brontosaurus
Trumpeting his bid for triumph
Distended in the middle
Like a bloated kidney bean

Sonny's sour spouse
Chases self-esteem
While Sonny languishes at her side
A bundle of mildewed dreams

The aging doe
Peddles gray platitudes
She plucked this morning
From the blue fungi
That flourish on the stroller
And smother the bassinet.

Meditation on a Son's Wedding Night

We were flat after the last farewell
Like a spinach soufflé
That failed to rise
Or a Hungry Jack pancake
Some zealous cook
Flipped the third time

Our hearts were thin as a Communion wafer
No beckoning gesture or invitation
Could make our bones blossom
The flesh grow full and firm
An invader had arrived
Armed to homestead the land
Carve out a corner
Stake her claim
A case of squatter's rights.

Sins of Omission: Remembrance for a Birthday

Sometimes all you remember
Are the mistakes you made
The things you didn't do
Those small sins
Of mother's omission
That can wear a hole in a child's heart

Like the time
He cried from 10 till 2
You shut the nursery door
Till all the tears dried up
You wonder if they left
Some permanent desert in the heart

Like the time you let
The waste in his diaper
Rub the bottom raw
Because you felt that day
Your life must have a purpose
Beyond Pampers and strained peas

Like the time you hit him
Because you hated yourself
A single tear cruised down his cheek
So lonely all he said was
I do good
In school Mom

Like the time his allergy kicked up
It was there
Where were you
Cruising down the highway
From one part-time job to the next
Trying to prove
What
It's hard to remember—now

Like all the things he did and said
To show he wasn't second best
To prove he wasn't
One step behind Number One and Number Three
Trying so hard, too hard
To carve out his place

Sometimes you wonder
If what makes him special
Is that he grew up
Not because of what you did
And didn't do
But in spite of what you did
And didn't do
And then you know

That makes him special
The core of strength
Inside his heart
Belongs to him
Sometimes the race is not
To those first front runners
But to those who feel they come from behind
And finally run free.

Marital Understudy

She seized her golden moment
Of ivory tulle and lace
Silver gravy ladles and look alike split levels
In *Little Mary's Garden*
An annual production
At Our Lady of Hope High

In the slippery sequel
Always on Call
The thud was soft
As velvet on a sliding runway
She auditioned for cameo roles
In *She Who Perseveres Till the End*
Then traded a manicured lawn and monogrammed sheets
For a one woman show.

Sonnet for an Unconceived Child

I was not a circle of mortar or an ellipse of cement
No one commissioned me
To flush the dead phrases from your drain pipe
No one claimed I'd coast to glory
If I let you drape me
Like a secondhand Raphael
Or a leftover Norman Rockwell
Over the blood stain on your bedroom wall

No one offered me overtime
To plug the abyss in your conversation
Smother precoital yawns
Extinguish the mushroom cloud of boredom
Trigger canned laughter on cue
No one.

No Familiar Moment

There's no familiar moment for the vacant stare
That shrouds the wing-backed chair
Like fog on the Golden Gate Bridge
No familiar moment for fluid to invade
The lung, cataracts to crust
The lens, waste to flood
The kidneys like undigested dung
No familiar moment for memories to thin
The heart to fail
No familiar moment to monitor
The baby's breath or the mother's respirator.

Aborting the Launch

She's here this morning
In the garden where I feed your sunflower
And nurse your fading cyclamen
These are favors
Any friend can perform
There are no life or death matters here
No prison sentence
Without parole

She's the letter in your Out basket
Forward - No Longer At This Address
Your recorded message "Sorry
The Professor is on sabbatical
All matters should be referred
To the Department"

She perches on your fence post
Like a freshly hatched starling
A non-swimmer on the rail
Of the Golden Gate Bridge
Reaching for our hands at that last half-second
Before the plunge.

The Land of Skulls

She died in a puddle
Of gray water and Cameo Cleanser
A woman who lived half a century
On her knees

They said an avalanche
Of something called plaque
Plowed through the door of her brain
Sweeping the floor of her soul clean

Of husbands drowning
In a sea of Scotch
Of daughters tap dancing to oblivion
In second rate chorus lines
Hemming other women's slips
Through bifocals thick as prison walls
Sleeping to the tune of typewriter keys
Orchestrated by the boss' eye

Of ladies of the house who left
Mildewed tile and dust balls
Windows caked with soot
For other women to scrape clean

Her world was a sea
Of scrub buckets and Oxydol
Lemon oil and boiled starch
Liberation was a dollar tip.

Dancing with Death

Impotence

The hungry eyes of old men
Plead for scraps
Fondling the freshly minted apple
Forever in the supermarket

The thirsty eyes of old men
Caress young flesh
With the finger tips
Of memory

The leaden eyes of old men
Solicit invitations
To a séance
On a distant afternoon.

Xmas Eve in Blackjack Town

Joe the Pit Boss appeared
Like a bill collector
From the cloud of Benson & Hedges
That hung above the table
Ready to swallow
Every ace and king

Mary Kay the Dealer
Spotted a boa constrictor
Easing his way
Through the dollar slot
Behold Joe snarled
Time to cough up suckers

It's Reno now
Not Sinai or Jerusalem
Good news swings
Off balance here
From a greased palm
And an agate eye.

The Year of Gambler's Anonymous

Love wore a number
Called 21
You could measure love
In Technicolor chips
Round dates on a calendar
Of seesawing odds

Love was 20
You could root your heart in that
Love was a pair of 8's
You could carve in two
Love was 11
You could mold that into magic
With a card some priest
Of luck had blessed

Love was a dealer's 6
Love was the house's 22
Love was a number that made you
Cinderella at the flick of a wand.

An Elegy to My Abdomen

In Memory of Anne Sexton's "In Celebration of my Uterus"

More is less
She stands before the full-length glass
Sucking in her gut
Searching for that hollow cave
Whose boundaries were the rib cage
And two sturdy pelvic bones

It reminds her of a window
You know the sort
The ones with cracked panes
And flaky grey paint

Or that can of imported Brie
Her son's future father-in-law blessed her with
The one whose lid exploded
Released an odor that insulted the air
Like the remains of last week's experiment
In Chem 101

It used to be a real kick
To pinch it
And get a low yield
Now the return on her investment
Is rich indeed
A spiraling dividend

Rolls and fistfuls
Of flesh
That feel like giant doughnuts
Left at yesterday's coffee break
Not time yet
To summon the mourners
Rehearse the dirge
Contact the crematorium
Or Your Friendly Embalmer
Not yet—but soon.

The Velvet Garrote

I make it a point to arrive at 7 A.M.
You'd be firing the electric log
In the Nob Hill suite
If it's March you'll be cruising the Bay

I feed Mother beef broth
Scrub out the grime between her toes
Clean her crotch
Stick a Q-tip in her ear

You'd be coasting at anchor in Sausalito now
Or maybe dipping escargot in spinach sauce on Fisherman's Wharf
Perhaps you're fondling a jade Buddha in Chinatown
Or worshipping the beach at Monterey

I'm fixing Mother breakfast
She doesn't eat bacon and eggs over easy
You mentioned the Eggs Sardou
That swim in uncurdled Hollandaise at the Top of the Mark

This morning I'll scour the toilet bowl
Scrape the ice box
Attack the oven with a Brillo pad
Bleach the brown stains on her pants

This must be the season
For long afternoons and cable car rides
For Grey Reisling in a Napa vineyard
For surfing in Santa Cruz and Sunday Brunch on the Tahoe Queen

I'll return precisely at 5
To see the dinner soup is warm
The saltines crisp and the Jell-o firm
No need to give it a second thought

It must be just about time for green velvet waves
To caress the beach at Carmel
I was reading Freud the other day
He says guilt can drive a man straight off the Golden Gate Bridge.

Terminal Dwelling

Her spirit's shrunk
To fit a dwelling
Unchosen
Such a diminutive prison

Its walls contract
The room diminishes
To a building block
In a child's nursery set

She fondles the furniture of greeting cards
Devours perfunctory get well wishes
Caressed with
Flawed precision

The carnation withers
The narcissus fade in a florist vase
A solitary iris languishes
In a dish garden gone dry

She knows one pronoun only
The importunate I
She extracts her tribute
In inelegant retreat.

Molotov Cocktail

They prepared me in the previous century
Those faces in the photograph
Whose liver was seared alive
In the acid of a thousand dry martinis
Who sampled a diet
Of laxatives and diuretics
Barbiturates designed
For those whose code was scrambled
At the ancestral tryst
My clock is set for detonation.

Sunset in Reno

Was it luck that left her
Impaled on the handle
Of a rusty slot machine
Her one good eye swimming
Uncertainly flawed at the center
Of a nickel cameo

Was it luck that left her
Embalmed at the blackjack table
A corpse come too soon
Arranged at random
On a homemade sarcophagus
Glued with odds and ends

Was it luck that left her
Clutching a spare card
Awaiting her partner
At the poker table
Fondling the knave of fantasy
A king of hearts, the royal flush

Was it luck that made her miss
That tinny Greyhound
The gamblers' special
Bent to bear her back
To a short order world of burgers
Soggy buns and synthetic fries?

The Going Away Party

Death's an unassuming guest
Arriving with arms outstretched
Laden with no inventory
Of B's that might have been A's
Gold stars on someone else's test
Ill-timed pregnancies, promotions missed
Clutching with glee no catalogue
Of burnt beefsteaks and dead connections.

Bogart's Hymn to Death

Time to close the curtain
Sweetie time to shut up shop
Time to leave 'em laughin'
Baby time to let the burden drop

Time to look the ghost of madness
Obliquely in the eye
Time to break the news
Angel all those dreams were lies

Time to pack your heater
Honey time to head out West
Time to wipe the good guys out
Everyone fails the test

Time to cut the devil in
Doll this hand is the last
Time to spin the wheel
Sister the future is the past.

Black Song for Billie Holiday

The night the blue saxophones died
You still remain in the spotlight's ivory heat
A riddle that puzzles the heart
Snatching from the soil of catastrophe
A nugget of perfect sound
Glowing like an iridescent candle
You breathe life into an embryo of song
Your eyes whisper a regal lament
That startles the heart
Yours was no Bourbon Street funeral.

Death of a Family Bakery

As I carve a path
Through the jungle of creditors' threats
Lay off notices, resignations
Legal briefs and bankruptcy forms
I remember my tenth birthday
The party with undrunk lemonade
Left over tollhouse cookies
Unblown whistles and horns
Party hats without heads
Favors no one took home

I was fresh from a New England village
Where the fate of an elm on Old Sudbury and Post
Became the Holy Grail
In someone's Crusade
I was a tollhouse and lemonade girl
A hat and horn kid

At California Country Day lemonade came laced
With maraschinos and grenadine
Mrs. Fields catered the cookies
Hats and horns arrived enshrined
In cellophane from Saks
Favors were handcrafted
By an artist who wintered in Scottsdale
Summered in Marin

My Mom squeezed fresh lemons
Rolled out worlds of cookie dough
We bought the crepe paper special at Safeway
Birthing a litter of lopsided baskets
Nodding rakishly at the guests
The invitations from Payless were uniform

RSVP
I can't come
I've got a golf lesson
A swimming meet at the Club
Soccer practice
A tennis match

Cal Country Day kids
Sipped guava punch
Nibbled mandarin orange and anisette bars
Preferred party hats without rubber bands
Favors and horns with the Hallmark label
So they resigned from my party

I never filed a brief or signed a form
No official notice in Sunny Success Land
I tried to play the game
With old rules
Cal Country Day kids don't yearn for real lemons or homemade horns
They crave exotic flavors and cookies with patent labels.

Hunting

In Memory of the Photographer Diane Arbus

She stalked them through the corridors
Of a sterile New Jersey clinic
Where keepers polished
Stainless steel locks
Massaged the bars
On rain streaked windows

Freaks and circus clowns
Transvestites wearing
Harlequin patches on their hearts
Down syndrome souls with broad faced genes
Eyes alive with love
Naked windows in the attic of our house

She'd seen enough of finely carved mannequins
Battling anorexia and crow's feet
Eyes suffocating in layers
Of shadow and mascara
To know the camera can abet the lie
Or lay bare the wound of truth.

Off Limits

It's time to establish a wildlife refuge
In the skirmish with creeping asphalt
A soaring shopping plaza
And seven identical motels
An endangered species can't reserve
The honeymoon suite at the Hyatt
Or dine at a restaurant that spins
On the tower of the Holiday Inn

A sandpiper pecks with genteel grace
At the emerald algae that coat
The few unblasted stones where the sea
Left her signature last week
Dotting the beach like grey ellipses
It's imperative to close the border
Seal off the area and mount a sign
Hunters will be prosecuted
Trespassers shot.

Octopus

She shall be a daughter forever
Entombed in the belly of the devilfish
He shall feed on her flesh
In the ink of night
His tentacles shall suck blood
From the chambers of her soul

Through caverns of coral
In incestuous seas
He shall pursue her
No flicker of love shall live
In his shadow
He shall possess her
Till her bones are bare
Her heart a hollow skull.

Blood on Ice

She is a figure frozen
In a crystal avalanche
A cameo entombed in ice
Foreplay is a silent reel spinning
In slow motion

Her breasts are a Kansas wheat field
Trapped in a drought
The eyes are glaciers sealed
Twin stalagmites dedicated
To a god of primal frost

No pyrotechnic burst can shatter
An iceberg buried
In the heart of the Bering Sea
Where no current quickens the core
Blood becomes a diamond mine
As the bright leaf droops in the dust.

Bipolar

The hairs on his leg are gold threads
A net of filigree woven on red brown silk
His chest a boxer's arena
With muscles poised
Like a premier danseur
Waiting to enter the ring

His finger tips caress dry flesh
That vibrates like a harp
Tuned to sing
At a master's breath

Her breasts are cradled in the sand
Twin orbs whose emblem will vanish
Like grains in an hourglass
Her eyes are globes of blue fire
Murmuring a secret long shared
Messengers of unacknowledged desire

I watch their bodies beckon
Like an iridescent channel
Inviting embarkation
On a new late evening breeze
Charged valences in equilibrium
Magnets of equal strength.

A Time to Reap

My soul is a grenade
That has exploded in my hand
The bones vaporize
And flesh drips
Into a plastic hour glass
That melts like a stubby candle

I was a snow bank
A rocky glacier shrouded
In an obscure and distant cradle
Now I am subliming
In a mist so thin
No hand will grasp it.

The Coroner's Report

Our investigation disclosed no sharply etched memories
True she did dislike duets
Abhorred skating in pairs
Preferred the ball machine to a partner on the courts
Always teed off alone
Single handed her sloop at sunset

She jogged on abandoned beaches and walkways declared unsound
Cycled the back paths only
Hiked unmarked trails
Spread her sleeping bag beside seldom visited streams

While others honed thc flutter kick
Rounded an arc in their back stroke
She plunged into the trough at the center
Where the present enters a conduit with no exit.

Shadow in an Anorexic Glass

My ribs are needles now
Sharp and exquisitely fine
Soon I shall be a sheet of cellophane
They will see me as a window
To contemplate a shrinking heart
Whose chambers house dwarfs
Refugees from Belsen
Mannequins in a cruise display at Saks

I shall pirouette in the shadow
A needle of light
Diminished to a period
At the end of a parchment treatise
Spread in the Mojave sun
I shall model a shroud so transparent
The designer's hand will grasp
A cage of flesh subliming.

Topography for a Bulimic

I live in a land with
Valleys of chocolate nougat
A mountain of croissants
Rivers of raspberry jam
I live in a house whose
Walls are built of cherry pie
I live in a room where
A starved heart is the cistern
I empty daily
With a finger tip.

Self-Portrait

I know Narcissus well
A banal but urbane figure
Presiding over a borrowed phrase
Peddler of second hand aphorisms

I'm told he succumbed
In a vacuum of bliss
A last tête-à-tête in monochrome
With his only paramour

Not that forlorn nymph
The echo of his eye
Poised at the distance he demanded
Charted to skirt the perils
Of a spotlight shared
Upstaging by some victor
In the pole vault for a golden statuette
A medallion etched in ivory

He slipped into that stagnant pool
Sure of his billing
Forever at the center
Of a one man show.

Janus

This sunflower
Whose roots pound against the dime store pot
Like the fists of babies trapped
In amniotic sacs
Longing for transplantation, light, and love
You are this.

This cyclamen
Enshrined in the kitchen sink like a recluse
Sipping with fastidious discipline
Stray drops of tap water
Shrinking from the sun's assault
You are this.

Beaching the Pod

Only two remain alive
Some say they're false
Black Pacific baleens
Half starved and dry
With parasites fawning
On the small intestine

Wheezing like old vagrants with catarrh
They paw the sand with impotent flippers
In a world too heavy to hold
Where blow holes sag
And stomachs implode
Where victory is not to the great of heart.

Requiem for a Dead Possibility

I met her last night
I sat across from her
In a commuter crowded alcove
At the Holiday Inn bar

I watched her grey eyes
As she cradled
A glass of Chardonnay
With the exquisite grace
Of a premiere danseuse
Charting her limits

I see them together
As they launch a kayak
Provision a raft for the American River
I watch them glide
In a perfect arc at Sun Valley
Down a sea of diamond snow

I see them scale
The north face of Half Dome
I watch them plant their tent
On the floor of Yosemite Valley
Beneath a redwood
In Kings Canyon

I see them brace their bodies
Against a noon wind on the Bay
As they unfurl a foresail
Trim the mizzen
Tune some rigging
On a salt sprayed deck

I see them hike
The switchback trail in Big Sur
I watch them pause
As the child rescues a fallen leaf
Pull taut the day pack straps
Then round the definitive loop

I met her last night
I sat across from her
During an academic discussion
Of chapter deadlines
Her body was an album
A telescope of possibility
Last night I met a set of grey eyes
The girl my son didn't marry.

Epitaph for a Flying Buttress

The obituary was careful to quote
Her friends "She was always supportive
And conscientious, a regular trooper"
The second pillar from the right
In a Greek temple
The third flying buttress from the left
In a Gothic cathedral
Like an ambulatory ear she understood when
You said "Take two aspirin
And call me in the morning"
She was the kind you count on when
Your mother spars with cardiac arrest
Or your wife battles breast cancer
She was the type you turn to when
The Savings and Loan fails or your husband has
An affair or your dog breaks his leg
Or your cat gets trapped in a tree
She wouldn't know what to do
With a fifth of Tequila, a bottle of Valium
Or a handgun.

Personal Effects

At the nursing home I found nothing
But bingo prizes, dime store
Necklaces, bargain basement
Cards with Mary and Jesus
Fireplaces and Santa Claus
Jars of generic hand lotion
A stuffed puppy with one eye
Dry leaves in an autumn field
Horoscopes for a winter season.

Chameleon

Her friends complained of sudden wind shifts
Abrupt alterations in the air current, colors
That changed like a high speed kaleidoscope
A compass needle spinning like a slowly advancing
Avalanche fueled by rage or terror or desire
To win the Good Housekeeping Seal of Approval
No one was ever sure
She stood in the path of ordinary disaster
Like a skyscraper on landfill
When she dissolved, no one noticed
The vacant lots she had inhabited
None of them long enough.

Over the Edge

Sometimes it takes small moments
A gnat circling the ear lobe
With gentle relentlessness
Like a bomber at Nagasaki
Birthday cards sent to friends
Who received them like stars
Punctual in a Tahitian sky
The smile in the morning mirror
Carved in apple cheeks and offered
With eagerness to every passerby
Phone messages mounting
To a dull crescendo no one hears
Till midnight when the stone
Rolls into the sea and the muzzle
In the mouth explodes.

The Good Matador

At his funeral their friends said
She played the perfect wife
Like a middle-aged virtuoso
But we were family and we knew
Veronica was more than
A bit player or a walk-on
She knew when to face the bull
At the instant when he'd paw
The furrows in their ring and lower
His head for the charge she'd start
Waving the cape, ever so slowly,
Unfolding the failures, one by one
She'd spread them before him
One at a time, ever so slowly,
Till he greeted the sword with relief.

Splitting the Circle

The Fencing Lesson

Humor's the best defense
No wall or moat is more effective
Once intimacy gets beyond the gates
No castle is the same

You must anticipate a thrust
Then drive your poniard home
The intruder will get the point
And your audience will call it wit

Be sure to graze the skin
A pinprick will do
Avoid the black eye
And bloody nose
Raw bruises mute the applause
You can't afford to forfeit an ovation.

A Mini Course in Grammar

"I" is a lonely pronoun
Sometimes
"You" demands
A subtle shift of focus

Third person
Distances quite well
Yet there's a curious coldness about it
Sometimes

"We" is rather cozy
Don't you think
Of course we forfeit our claim
To the unique status we covet
Sometimes.

The Exorcism of Antiques

You've met them both you know
That boy and girl from long ago
That darling twinkle toes
Tap dancing determinedly
Sweating like a stevedore
A smile slapped between her dimples
Like a slab of adhesive tape
Palm outstretched to snatch stray pennies, a bouquet of A's
Or love.

You've met him too
That middle boy
Slapped like some forlorn salami between two halves
Of a homebaked croissant
Replacing burnt-out tubes in daddy's Philco
Beefing up the family album
Labeling toys for Mama's garage sale
Making his bid for a nod.

Readily Transferable Skill

Exorcising words
Like sin and fail
Is a full time job
A steady occupation
No need to worry
About shorter work weeks or a lay off

Then there's the overtime
Especially at 4 A.M.
The sweat stained pillow and rumbling belly
The dream of sprinting down Main Street
Minus your pants and bra
A strobe snapping at your heels.

The Spectre of Success

A jackpot's the judgment bell
Who needs blackjack
The full house and royal flush
Suck joy from the morning
Leaving knots in the gut
Chunks of half-digested vomit

I watched the Berkeley Bag Lady
Discover half of someone's hot dog
She shared it with the Balloon Lady
Polka Dot Willie and the Bubble Man
They painted the portal of Sather Gate
With leftover mustard and relish

Decorated the steps
Of Sproul Hall
With pickles and wilted lettuce
Then curled up in the same sleeping bag
Clutching the same lucky penny
On a pillow of sunshine and cheeseburgers.

The Ledger

Fantasy is a spendthrift
It squanders our gifts
Assuring us a daydream's
Sufficient payment

Hoarders lose,
Harboring too little faith
Too much fear
A blemish mars the praise.

Recipe

This is Death Valley
It depends how far you plant your tap root
If you sink it long and deep
You'll survive

If you want to hug the surface
And always see the sun
Explode above you
Like a fire ball at Nagasaki
You'll sublime like a snow bank
In an early Tahoe Spring.

The Chimes of Partch

They're tuned to a scale
You can't discover on a Steinway
Priam heard its voice
Before trumpets called at Troy
Leonidas listened to their magic
Before Xerxes marched to Thermopylae
Their echo rings
In Uganda and Zimbabwe
Where five tones utter volumes
No scroll or tome can capture.

In what tongue do they speak to me?
A claustrophobic dweller
In a California condo
Drowning in a sea of Heavy Metal
Canned laughter on Newhart and Cheers
Science is clay
With no breath of magic
We grow deaf with no echo of the past.

Stairs

We've lost our entrance
Mislaid it in our march
Elevators and escalators
Can't replace it
Swing wide the heart of Rome
Ascend its seven hills

Stairs traveled with Roman legions
A gate that led to glory
Sharing the terrain
In a romance with memory

The Aracoeli was a door to wonder
Better to caress the tip of heaven
Than languish on the plateau
Climbing was a prayer
Unlocking a realm that pilgrims craved
The rungs on Jacob's ladder

The Cordonata lifted the curtain for a palace
Ushered in an Emperor
There are no kings on the Los Angeles freeway
We live on an arid plain.

Elegy

Memory's an importunate guest
Arriving uninvited
Laden with dubious baggage
A litter of odds and ends

It strews hybrid treasure
On a pale shroud
Its synchrony not unalloyed
With dissonance

We snatch small moments
Hoping for gifts not subject to scale or tithe
The brief smile
A clasped hand
That flash fire of difference
Forged in a common crucible

Not base metal
Perhaps the philosopher's stone
Its elixir transient
An echo thin as a thread
Maybe a panacea
For all too short a season
Our gold filament of immortality
A blossom in the dust.

Tracking the Florida Black Panther

The Fish and Game Commission christened him #10
They gave him a radio collar for a birthday present
He's one of 20 now
A mama's boy the trackers say
Reluctant to snare the armadillo or devour the fawn
Wary of his mother's breeding

When her mate arrives
She'll drive him from the Strand
Demand he win his way alone
Wolfe claimed you can't go home again
When the point's not going or coming
But learning how to leave.

The Blind Dog Who Sleeps on the Blue Settee

His eyes are opaque
Like grey marbles no one wanted
To trade in the Spring shoot
His leg is a blade of granite
Planted in gallant despair
On a floor of faded velvet

He sleeps in a cradle of urine
In the cave of the blue settee
Dreaming of the sapphire ring
The morning he scaled Half Dome
Crowning El Capitan
His legs pulsing like the earth
In a dawn tremor
He held a halo of fire in his hand
Vowing to live forever
In a house bathed in blue light.

Marching to a New Drummer

The Writer's Sonnet

It is hazardous
To burrow long
In a tunnel this systolic
Best to retreat
Above ground
To a garden overgrown
With familiar weeds
Apples bruised in the Fall

You risk implosion
In a retort this rarefied
It's an atmosphere too thin
A vacuum with
Obscure boundaries overcharged
By the electric emptiness of self scrutiny.

The Writer's Wet Suit

I am the Sea of Cortez
The sea Steinbeck plunged in whole
In search of rare anemones
Whispering of flesh and purple fields
Bodies bending
Like windflowers at our touch

Arms that draw us
Toward a mouth
That swallows spirits whole
And feasts in bliss on their marrow.

The Poet as Voyeur

I'm a Peeping Tom
At wedding receptions
I carve dolls' houses
People them with miscarriages
Trial separations
Alimony payments, visitation rights

At funerals I plant myself among the mourners
Imagining the widow's glee
At slipping the knot
Of hypodermic needles and stained sheets
The daughter-in-law's dismay
That the spare bedroom won't be vacant next Fall

I'm at my best
In crowds for all occasions
I slip into someone's tapestry
Take up residence
In a second hand skin
I am a giant eye.

The Writer at Half Past Five

Every word dipped in blood
Marinated in sweat, seasoned with doubt
I draped a comma in a commemorative flag
When the clock chimed half past four

You enshrine a semicolon
Canonize a verb
Beatify some errant phrase
When the seconds stretch like rubber bands
Then snap, boomerang, and ricochet
Hurling you back on the blank page

Every sentence is etched in acid
We chisel them from the marrow of our bones
Every stanza's carved in some corner of the heart
Awaiting a nod, a smile, an unsolicited embrace
We fling wide our arms and grasp at air
Hunger and thirst for living flesh
Starved on a diet of prepositions
We lust after the key in the lock, the familiar face in the door frame.

The Muses and Their Progeny

They enter on tiptoe
Arriving from some minefield in the heart
Sometimes in bundles or in pairs
Occasionally a solitary wanderer
Who strayed from the pack
Come to map uncharted habitats
Irrigate a desert or carve settlements in the wilderness
Bent on colonizing the outback of imagination.

Favorite Son

You are an antenna finely tuned
A fisherman whose hook is baited
To capture the flame of an evening smile
You are a chisel sharply honed
To excavate a dream of love
Etched in the heart
You are a touchstone
To you the magic of silence speaks.

Ancestral Chorale from Wales

The echo is seasoned with choirboys
Whose wide-eyed notes were the wick
That lit a thousand faces in the mines
Of a land where the day star was subterranean

Where men whose eyes creased
In their dawn
Whose shoulders buckled early
In the battle
Burnt incense before their sons
Before the diamond C dissolved
In a spongy lung dusted
With bitumen flakes
My heart scales the mountain of their song
So rarely each fresh ascent is an Austerlitz
Their fathers fertilized the soil
Where a gene to rappel
Took root.

Learning to Play in the Symphony

Cancer and the Southern Cross

At the tips of the cross
They beckon
Those four invincible beacons
Flinging wide their shaft of light
Keepers of the harbor
Where you know the voyage ends

They split the fog
Swallow whole the radioactive wind
They whisper the node of cells
That spreads its shroud across your lung
Cannot smother the heart
Or invade the terrain where courage dwells

They summon you to a tournament
Where a determined jouster earns the laurel wreath
They invite you to a banquet of light
Spread in the shadow of a cross.

A Crack in the Plain

A half century ago I planted my hand
On the breast of Oklahoma
I rooted it there in the Great Plain
The soil was black as bitumen
But the fistful I seized was dusted
With globes of dew

Yesterday I set the fingers on the clock
Forward and spread my hand across its face
There I tracked those cracks
Lacing the dusty clay
Announcing the waning of my cycle
Messengers from a dry season.

Marketing Fear

How about a trip to hell this season?
You can package and peddle that
You can sell Death Valley
There's something out there that speaks to us
The dragon beneath the gates
Camouflaged in whispers of cloudless skies
Brushing an horizon
Immeasurably distant and vast

Tread lightly on its spine
You may suck water from its stones
But beneath that rock
A serpent dwells
While the buzzard hovers low
Waiting to caress a fresh nocturnal skull

It soared to 134 degrees
The year before the Great War
The desert was a wonder and a weapon then
A land of gold, silver, copper
Charcoal and talc
Where clay moguls sold their soul
For a ton of ice in rhyolite
And men mined borax for a buck fifty a day.

A Vision of Omaha Beach:
D-Day June 6, 1944

A flag droops at the foot of Diamond Head
Eclipsed by a thousand flares
That set ablaze a bleak uncertain shore
Like Roman candles in the Harbor they called Pearl

Soon the flag will cease
To court ambivalence and despair
It will lift again
A bruised and ragged hand
Striving to embrace a sky
Laced with blue stars

There will be carnage on the beaches and the fields
But death will then be seasoned
With the blessed absence of ambiguity
Anzio will be a diamond
Mined in some distant Eden
Far from My Lai and Saigon

They will scale the cliffs at Omaha
With a purpose fixed and constant as Polaris
Their blood will irrigate stones
Bring forth the rose of freedom
Bathed in pain
Cleansed in the fire of resurrection.

Defacing Mount Rushmore

You want to carve Coolidge
Next to the Great Emancipator
Or whatever the fans at Ford's called him
After he was shot
Ol' Cal would be better than Warren G
But imagine him at San Juan Hill
Holed up at Valley Forge
Or sweating out the last 10 lines of the Declaration

We're down to Hoover
Eisenhower and Ford
But they didn't plant a putting green
On the plains of Monticello
Or tighten their belts in the Continental Congress
We could carve him cutting school lunches
Slipping a grenade to a Contra
Or kissing the tomb of a Luftwaffe ace at Bitborg.

Survivor:
Midnight Sonnet for the Homeless on Market Street

The connoisseurs of Charpentier
Liszt and Debussy
Stroll toward the grey cells
Labeled Benz and BMW
Cradling the corpse
Of a Grand Marnier soufflé
An empty goblet of Cabernet
A snifter of Drambuie

The ragged hot dog perches on her stick
Like the banner Lee bore at Gettysburg
A raw tomato floats
In a lettuce leaf boat
Sinking with battered but genteel grace
On a dead sea of Diet Coke.

Sirocco:
Wind Song for the Homeless on Market Street

Night sentinels police their heart
Worshippers of Sutherland
Pavarotti's devotees
Disciples of Balanchine
Baryshnikov and Kirkland
March past them dreaming
Of that rare filet at the Fairmont
A flute of Chardonnay
An Amaretto demitasse
Some B&B on ice

They shove their supermarket cart
Through the desert of Market Street
Cradling a limp MacBLT
Plucked from an aging puddle
The Hefty bag in their Safeway cart shrinks
Like gums in a toothless skull
Tonight the wind will singe their flesh
Nestle in their throat like a torch.

Confronting AIDS

Your raw heart belongs to me
It's community property
I hear it pulse
When ambulance sirens slice the air
And paramedics smother a yawn
As they deliver their midnight cargo

Those crippled cells you can't claim alone
They're lodged in the chambers of my heart
Where labels like syndrome and sarcoma
Are blank as a forgotten Christmas tag
This plague's no island
Where you'll cluster like haunted lepers
It's the Cyclops whose eye
We'll pluck as one.

HIV

We have an interest in raw hearts
They're community property
When ambulance sirens slice
The air and medics unload their cargo
We own stock in Molokai
Where we'll make a trophy of that Cyclops
Whose eye we pluck as one.

AIDS Through a Telescope on Mount Blanc

You were a disease
Declared invincible
Two centuries ago
They conquered you
Autocrat of wind and ice
They invaded your cradle of death

The physician Paccard
Balmat a carver of crystal
Battling an epidemic of height with sticks
Haversacks and a barometer
They stamped their seal of triumph
With the sole of a hobnail boot
A thunderclap of hands
On your frozen wounds

They scaled glaciers
Sliced trails
Through fields of ice
They jousted with banks of ivory fog

I watch now through an artificial eye
Breathe life
On the summit
Of their courage.

Traveling Beyond Definition

Normal,
What does it mean?
Belting base hits for Dad
In a Little League skirmish
Snickering at the sissy
Who sketched a fly so real
You could watch its wings soar
Who carved a seal with blue black eyes
Whispering of starfish and sea foam
Beckoning beyond the harbor

Normal,
What does it mean?
Sucking a girl's nipple
Stroking with sweaty palms
Telling the guys in the dorm
You scored again last night
Howling for the home team
In the NFL Play Off
Declaring ballet
An endangered species

Normal,
What does it mean?
Hoarding hugs and kisses
For Mom and Sister Sue
Reserving a handshake for Dad
Mounting a fake moosehead on the mantle
Instead of Renoir or Raphael
Polishing tarnished boxing trophies
Trading pink dust ruffles
For a black and white spread

Normal,
What does it mean?
Assigning girls to the boysenberry pie
And brownie shift
Bringing Budweiser and bourbon to the cook out
Is normal John Wayne,
Or W. H. Auden?
Gertrude Stein,
Or Marilyn Monroe?
Elizabeth Barrett Browning, or Adrienne Rich?

If normal's straight,
Is gay crooked?
A lopsided detour or premature dead end
On a road map run amuck
A con man on the lam
A stick some half blind whittler bungled

Is gay a trickle of thin hormones
Flowing in the wrong stream
A planet spinning out of orbit
A dwarfed dad cowering in the shadow
Of Good Ol' Dominant Mom
Is gay love locked in silence?
Or is normal the warm hand of a friend
Clasped in the Gay Freedom Day Parade?

A Stranger Called Alzheimer

A filament of acid swells in my brain
Merely a trickle now they say
Soon it will crest at full flood
Etch caves and precipices in each cell and lobe
Erode the trail of memory
Till the face in the mirror
Earns no nod
Or flicker of familiarity

Till the man whose body has met mine
Means as much no more
Than the homeless vagrant
Hunched behind a pillar
In the colonnade at City Hall
Till the steps to my apartment
Are a Chinese puzzle
And I live in an uncharted land
With a stranger called myself.

The Average Heart

The chambers of the average heart
Pulse in rhythm with the metronome
Of standard expectations
The chambers of the average heart
Are lined with customary velvet
Laced with the vein
Of children's recitals
A familiar breath at 4 A.M.
The Xmas card with a family portrait

The diseased heart is a sponge
Whose valves leak at the whisper
Of an eyelash
Cushioned in straw and bamboo
Creased with the seam
Of noon wine
The ivory heat of a midnight sun
A floodlight seasoned with a throat of sand
The nightmare in a naked eye.

Case History of a Terrorist

Our preliminary examination of the patient
Reveals no abnormality
True he spent hours at the zoo
At one with the cheetah policing his cage
On friendly terms with a polar bear
Pacing like Napoleon from one smooth stone to the next

Admittedly he shared intimate secrets with his Doberman
Whom he cited as user friendly
We acknowledge that he filed its incisors
Till they carved an abyss the size of a grenade
In the field of the nursery floor

At day care he staked out his sand castle
With a steel tape and a marble eye
He wooed his second wife with a treatise
And courted the third with a slogan
Secretions however do seem to unnerve him
Sweat, semen, tears.

Sheltering the Enemy

You invade my territory
Marching in like some usurper
Armed to homestead the land
Carve out your corner
Stake your claim
Plead your case for squatter's rights

What's your weapon anyway
The tropic core beneath that crust of ice
The electric eye that links with mine
And burrows out secrets buried there
The tongue of honey that can season
Inauthentic brass with the elixir of eloquence
The arm that inches within stalking distance
As we discuss the merits of your recent novel
In the corner of a bookstore

I should evict you from this house
You're no fit tenant for a landlord turned fifty
You and this feeling that I'm twenty
And ripe to launch my skiff on an uncertain sea
Where the tide will never ebb or the wind subside
Where the moon will wax out of season
And you and I will beach this boat on an island
Where we'll waltz beneath a crystal chandelier
In some exotic ballroom
Where the fingers on the clocks are frozen.

Plutonium 235

They cluster like obese children
In the shelter of the La Brea Tar Pit
Struck by a bolt of wonder
In the midst of trees bare now
Of leaves so delicious
They once dripped fragrant phlegm

This globe of fire has shattered roots
Distant from their vision
Yet with volcanic winds it lashes their back
And drives their faces forward
To a doom triggered by thumbnails and a chip of sand.

The Wheat Fields of Chernobyl

Will you be now
A land without eagles
Where wrens and sparrows
Find no solitary bough
Or limb unscarred
By a rain of ashes

Will your children claw the fields for bread
And find there only dust
Will wombs be vacant
And marrow sterile
Will your roses bloom only in memory
And your lilies vanish from the field?

In the Shadow of Lassen Volcano

They're hermits by choice
The whitebark pine and pika
Mountain hemlock, pinemat manzanita
Bog Kalmia and pink heather

They hug the earth
Trap air on the fringe of a leaf
Cluster in tiny colonies to beat back layers of wind
Creep down the slope for cover

No brushing the planets
With their finger tips
They feed on a diet
Calculated to conserve
While we mass along the lip
Of a crater about to buckle
A crust that sags
Beneath our weight.

Tenting in Lassen Forest

How would the pine and fir awake
The flowering beds of volcanic rock
In a world without Winnebagos and dome tents
No Styrofoam coolers stuffed
With ballpark franks and Chianti
Safeway bags sagging with S and W beans
Garbage cans and Coleman stoves
Flashlights and diesel fumes

In what world would the antelope and black tail
The mule deer breathe and drink the sun
Without Folgers Instant and corned beef hash
Plastic spoons and paper towels

In what liquid world would the Eagle Lake trout
The Kohanee salmon glide
Dodging no baited hooks and lines
Gripped by the hand of a species
Battling crack
Returned to a world
Whose body they remodeled
Whose face they cosmetized?

The Last Frontier

It is possible
To trigger this final conquest
With a single christy turn
Provided we draft the will
To traverse slopes labeled
Out of bounds

To sever yellow warning tape
Decapitate slender poles that
Like lone sentinels separate machine groomed streets
From virgin land where we
Not some high priest worshipping
At the altar of a monitor
Carve the lanes
And make the traffic rules

Where the snap of a boot strap
Or the wave of a pole
Through air charged with the voltage
Of civilized despair

Coursing through pine and spruce
Ignite the crescendo of our echo
Avalanche
Proclaims us rulers
Of the mountain whose answer
Defies prediction.

Aging on an Island of the Young

The grey heron hunts at evening
Soaring like an arrow through the midnight air
A tawny owl pierces the blue black sky
With strength stored in the heart
Of those who know the night
The Arctic fox, the homely slug

Eels feast in an ebony sea
Unlocking riddles with the key of depth
Not speed
The lacewing and Roe fawn
The possum and the badger
Cohabit with a waning moon

Orb web spiders cradle in a shrinking belly
Silken threads to spin a world
The bush cricket chirps in tones unheard
In a land where collagen rules
The lynx sprints with greatest zest at dusk
The swan glides with full throated grace on the kiss of evening air

The common crayfish and caddis fly
The otter and the snail
Speak with Venus
Share secrets with Orion's belt
The starfish and the sea urchin
Embrace the setting sun

Dolphins dance their pas de deux
With joy in a fading light
The octopus spreads nocturnal tentacles
Wide enough to hold a world
The desert flower's evening root sinks deep and true
Growing old is a cosmic art.

A Trail to Wounded Knee:
A Sonnet in Honor of Chief Crazy Horse

They clustered along the lip
Of the bowl called
Little Bighorn
Sioux warrior, Cheyenne chief,
The braves of Arapaho
Prepared to shatter the gloved fists
And booted thighs
Massed in the knoll of Medicine Trail

Relic seekers track their fire now
On discs and painted monitors
Souvenir mongers count the threads in that noose
He wove to fit the throat
Of a Man who rode for glory
A moat in the Great Spirit's eye.

Victory Song at the Custer Monument

You led them to the lip
Of a bowl called Little Bighorn
Chiefs, warriors, braves
You breathed into their spirit
A will of steel
To shatter a fortress of raped land
Slaughtered buffalo

Souvenir seekers bow their head
Before a stone planted
In memory of the man who fought for glory
No marker for you
Strategist of justice
Engineer of victory.

The Song of Popul Vuh

At first there was no chant
Only calm and stillness
A vast dome
Dark and empty
Motionless and silent
In the night

We offered young blood to the gods
To insure the best
A place in heaven
We beheaded the vanquished warrior
So he would not eat salt
In a dry season

Our legacy lives
In the streets of San Salvador
The swamps of Honduras
A jungle in Guatemala
The Contras bear our banner
The Sandinistas invoke our name.

Vintage Matrimony

A Cabernet well tended
Ripens as it ages in the cask
Tapping the contents too soon
Weakens the thread of longevity

Let laughter mellow the tannin
Enrich a fragile bouquet
Sip slowly the fruit of the harvest
No offering from a raw season.

The Mother-in-Law's Lament

Did you ever meet the sort of girl
You wish your son married
That pluperfect porcelain elf
Who'd fly fish on the shore
While he kayaked down the rapids
Or rafted the river's fork
Who'd match him mogul for mogul
In the skiers' steeple chase?

Who'd fire out five grandkids
Like a hyperactive cannon
Who'd iron his shorts
And starch his sheets
Who'd scrub his toilet bowl
With zest

Who'd hitch her covered wagon
To the star of Sonny's needs
While churning out a cheese soufflé
Or tending the Eternal Flame
Beneath his cherries jubilee
An Elaine worthy of our Launcelot

The sort of girl who'd spot on cue
The paragon you produced
Who'd embrace each piece of spare advice
Like a chip from the Holy Grail
While pumping peas into Sonny's son
And vacuuming with glee

The sort of girl
Who'd recognize
The rights of prior tenants
The sort of girl
You could spend
The rest of his life with.

The Ski Slope at Sunset

The mountain is a sea of diamonds now
I must wedge with care
Carve triangles and parentheses
I must glide toward the scotch pine
And a blue spruce
I must arc in slow parabolas now at mid century.

Mid Life Passage

A field long fallow now blooms
A chamber long sealed now splits its lock
The wall of an earthen dam now swells
As the fist of courage pounds and presses
Releasing mist that irrigates
A parched and barren land.

The Merits of Dining at Home

I'm used to the way you barbeque a London broil
To our thirty-three-year division of labor
You with the Hills Brothers and scrambled eggs
Me with the corn flakes and toast
The ham and swiss you pack for lunch
The reminder to take my calcium and vitamin C
Homely skills without which my house would be
Famine prone

In their place this romance offers a liquid diet
To a fifty year old used to solid fare
A soufflé of "if's" and "suppose's"
Ready to fall before it rises
A meringue of "maybe's" and "possibly's"
Designed to shrink the thighs of a linebacker
To the ankles of a ballerina
Enough to make Helen of Troy think twice
And Bathsheba reconsider.

Jettisoning at Fifty

The mast is cracked
The hull's sprung a leak,
Time to pack the sea biscuits
Fill the last canteen

When the radiator boils
In the middle of the Mojave
And a tire blows
On the back road to Tuolumne
You attend to the trail mix
And put aside the Chablis

When there's more time behind
And less ahead
You read the bold print
And let the footnotes be.

Twentieth-Century Triptych

Panel I

Amelia Earhart: The First Woman to Fly the Atlantic Ocean

You became Daedalus' daughter
After the Aegean captured Icarus
You cut through clouds
Soared above the sun
You were mistress of the wind
Stamping your seal on the stars.

Panel II

Gertrude Ederle: The First Woman to Swim the English Channel

They titled you true
Gertrude with the mighty thigh
You hurled your spear at the waters
Between Dover and Calais
You thrust it toward that point of land
You would call your own,
You were Artemis riding the waves.

Panel III

Eleanor Bachman: The White Mistress of Jack Johnson, the first Black Heavyweight Champion of the World, who retained his title in a match with Jim Jeffries, "The Great White Hope," in Reno, Nevada, on July 4, 1910

What trophy's left for you
Another Helen
Poised between black Paris
And white Menelaus,
One more piece of disputed ground
In a holy war
Whose battlefield was Reno
On a dry and dusty night

Your bards were Cincinnati Slim
And the Sundance Kid
Your rally cry was Forty Rounds
Or Die
Jack kept his belt
What trophy's left for you?

Acknowledgments

Many of the poems in this book appeared in the online chapbook *The Land of Skulls*, www.languageandculture.net, October 2006. These and other poems previously appeared as follows.

"Aborting the Launch" in *SpeedPoets* (Australia), Vol. 7.2.

"Aging on an Island of the Young" in *Ascent Aspirations Magazine* (Canada, online, Nov. 2007).

"Agape" in *SpeedPoets* (Australia), Vol. 7.5.

"AIDS Through a Telescope on Mount Blanc" in *SpeedPoets* (Australia), Vol. 6.6.

"Alice and Dorothy" in *cc&d (Children Churches & Daddies)*, vol. 192 (Jan. 2009); and *Ceremony, a journal of poetry and other arts* (2008).

"Ancestral Chorale from Wales" in *Ascent Aspirations Magazine* (Canada, online, May 2008); *The David Jones Society* (Wales, UK, 2009); *SpeedPoets* (Australia), Vol. 8.3; and *Poetalk* (Winter/Spring 2009).

"The Average Heart" in *SpeedPoets* (Australia), Vol. 7.1.

"Beaching the Pod" in *Jerry Jazz Musician: Poetry* (online); *Poet's Ink* (online, Nov. 2008); and *Ceremony, a journal of poetry and other arts* (2008).

"Bipolar" in *Sunken Lines*, no. 6 (online, Autumn 2006).

"Black Song for Billie Holiday" in *SpeedPoets* (Australia), vol. 7.7; *Jerry Jazz Musician: Poetry* (online); and *nthposition* (online, UK, Feb. 2009).

"The Blind Dog Who Sleeps on the Blue Settee" in *SpeedPoets* (Australia, 50th Birthday Issue, 2007); and *nthposition* (UK, online, March 2009).

"Blood on Ice" in *Sunken Lines*, no. 6 (online, Autumn 2006); and *The Journal* (once *of Contemporary Anglo-Scandinavian Poetry*), no. 17 (UK, Winter 2006/7).

"Bogart's Hymn to Death" in *Ceremony: a journal of poetry and other arts* (Spring 2009).

"Cancer and the Southern Cross" in *SpeedPoets* (Australia), Vol. 7.3; and *Thick With Conviction* (online, Apr. 2009).

"Case History of a Terrorist" in *Black Bear Review*, No.11 (Spring/Summer 1990).

"Chameleon" in *Concho River Review*, Vol. 22, No. 1 (Spring 2008).

"Confronting AIDS" in *Poetry San Francisco Quarterly* (n.d.)

"Corporate Spouse" in *SpeedPoets* (Australia), Vol. 7.7; *Ascent Aspirations Magazine* (Canada, online, Feb. 2009); and *Mannequin Envy* (Winter Melt Issue, Winter/Spring 2009).

"A Crack in the Plain" in *cc&d (Children Churches and Daddies)*, Vol. 164 (Sept. 2006).

"The Chimes of Partch" in *Ascent Aspirations Magazine* (Canada, online, Nov. 2007).

"The Coroner's Report" in *SpeedPoets* (Australia), Vol. 6.3; *Illogical Muse* (online, Summer 2007); *Thick With Conviction* (online, October 2008); and *nthposition* (online, UK, Feb. 2009).

"Death of a Family Bakery" in *Sunken Lines*, no. 6 (online, Autumn 2006).

"Defacing Mount Rushmore" in *Wide Open Magazine* (July 1986); and *Jerry Jazz Musician: Poetry* (online).

"Delivery Room" in *Ascent Aspirations Magazine* (Canada, online, May 2006).

"Diagnosis" in *SpeedPoets* (Australia), Vol. 7.8.

"Elegy" in *Ascent Aspirations Magazine* (Canada, online, Nov. 2007).

"An Elegy to My Abdomen" in *Ascent Aspirations Magazine* (Canada, online, Feb. 2009); *Blue Sky Bodyworks*, no. 10 (1987); and *Poet's Ink* (online, Mar. 2009).

"Epitaph for a Flying Buttress" in *Concho River Review*, Vol. 21, No. 1 (Spring 2007).

"Esperanto" in *SpeedPoets* (Australia), Vol. 7.1; and *Jerry Jazz Musician: Poetry* (online).

"The Exorcism of Antiques" in *SpeedPoets* (Australia), Vol. 7.6.

"Favorite Son" in *Shemom*, no. 26 (Fall/Winter 2006); and *Ascent Aspirations Magazine* (Canada, online, May 2009).

"The Fencing Lesson" in *Reach for the Stars* (1986 New Horizons Poetry Anthology).

"A Former Passion for 3's" in *Mannequin Envy* (online, Winter 2007); and Third Award, Redwood Acres Fair, Summer 1986.

"The Going Away Party" in *Sunken Lines*, no. 6 (online, Autumn 2006); and *Ceremony, a journal of poetry and other arts* (2008).

"The Good Matador" in *nthposition* (online, UK, Jan. 2007).

"The Harp at Birth" in *Ascent Aspirations Magazine* (Canada, online, May 2006).

"The Harp of Eros" in *Illogical Muse* (online, Summer 2007).

"HIV" in Jerry Jazz Musician: Poetry (online).

"Home on Mother's Day" in *SpeedPoets* (Australia), Vol. 7.7; and *nthposition* (UK, online, Feb. 2009).

"Hunting" in *Ascent Aspirations Magazine* (Canada, online, May 2008).

"Impotence" in *Hidden Oak*, (Fall/Winter 2008); *Foliate Oak* (online, Sept. 2008); *Poet's Espresso* (online, Sept. 2008); *The Poet's Haven* (online), no. 6; *Poetic Matrix* (online letter 6); *Pirene's Fountain* (online, Oct. 2008); *The Best of the Foliate Oak Online 2009 (Literary Journal)*; and *The Stray Branch* (Spring/Summer 2009).

"In the Shadow of Lassen Volcano" in *Black Bear Review*, No. 12 (Spring/Summer 1992).

"Janus" in *Poetic Hours*, no. 27 (UK, Autumn 2006); and *Jerry Jazz Musician: Poetry* (online).

"Jettisoning at Fifty" in *nthposition* (online, UK, June 2008).

"The Land of Skulls" in *Bay Area Poets Coalition* (February 1987), vol. 11, no. 8, First Prize (Category 3: Poet's Choice); *Visions*, no. 27 (Black Buzzard Press); Honorable Mention Award, *Black Buzzard Press*; *The Reach of Song, Book 7* (1988); E.M. Tanne Awa

"The Last Frontier" in *Miller's Pond Poetry Magazine* (online, Spring 2009).

"The Ledger" in *SpeedPoets* (Australia), Vol. 7.7; *Hidden Oak* (Fall/Winter 2008); *The Same*, Vol. 7, Nos. 1-2 (Summer/Fall 2008); and *The Poet's Haven*, no. 6 (online, 2008).

"Marital Understudy" in *The Dirty Napkin*, Vol. 2.1 (Winter 2009); and *Ceremony, a journal of poetry and other arts* (2008).

"Marketing Fear" in *Poetry Salzburg Review*, No. 12 (Autumn 2007).

"Meditation on a Son's Wedding Night" in *Shemom*, no. 30 (Spring 2008).

"The Merits of Dining at Home" in *Grasslands Review*, No. 3 (Spring 1990).

"Mid Life Passage" in *Ceremony, a journal of poetry and other arts* (2008); and *Dance of My Hands* (online).

"Miscarriage" in *SpeedPoets* (Australia), Vol. 6.3; *Poet's Ink* (online, Nov. 2008); and *nthposition* (online, UK, Feb. 2009).

"A Mini Course in Grammar" in *The Archer*, n.d.

"Molotov Cocktail" in *SpeedPoets* (Australia), Vol. 6.2; *Thick With Conviction* (online, Oct. 2008); and *nthposition* (online, UK, Feb. 2009).

"Mother and Daughter-in-Law: in *Shemom*, no. 30 (Spring 2008).

"The Mother-in-Law's Lament" in *Poet's Espresso* (online, Dec. 2008/Jan. 2009); *Wild Violet* (online), Vol. 7, No. 3; and *Ascent Aspirations Magazine* (Canada, online, Feb. 2009).

"The Muses and Their Progeny" in *Chip Off the Writer's Block*; *Poetic Matrix* (online letter 6, 2008); *The Poet's Haven*, no. 6 (online, 2008); *Miller's Pond Poetry Magazine*, Vol. 12, Issue 1 (online, Winter 2009); and *SpeedPoets* (Australia), Vol. 8.7.

"No Familiar Moment" in *Splizz*, Issue 63 (Wales, 2008); *Thick With Conviction* (online, Oct. 2008); and *SpeedPoets* (Australia), Vol. 8.6.

"Octopus" in *Poet's Espresso* (online, Oct./Nov. 2008); *The Poet's Haven*, no. 6 (online, 2008); *SpeedPoets* (Australia), Vol. 8.7; *Jones Av.* (Spring 2009); and *The Stray Branch* (Spring/Summer 2009).

"Off Limits" in *The Poet's Haven*, no. 6 (online, 2008); *Poet's Espresso* (online, Sept. 2008); *Miller's Pond Poetry Magazine*, Vol. 12, Issue 1 (online, Winter 2009); *Language and Culture (dot) net* (online, Summer/Fall 2009); and *SpeedPoets* (Australia), Vol. 8.8.

"Over the Edge" in *Current Accounts*, no. 25 (UK, Winter 2007/8); *Poetalk* (Winter/Spring 2008); and *Jerry Jazz Musician: Poetry* (online).

"Personal Effects" in *cc&d (Children Churches and Daddies)*, Vol. 165 (Oct. 2006).

"Plutonium 235" in *Ascent Aspirations Magazine* (Canada, online, May 2007).

"The Poet as Voyeur" in *Conditioned Response* (Dec. 1986).

"Prognosis" in *Drown In My Own Fears*, no. 7 (online, 2009); and *Mannequin Envy* (Winter Melt Issue, Winter/Spring 2009).

"Readily Transferable Skill" in *Ascent Aspirations Magazine* (Canada, online, May 2007).

"Recipe" in *Poet's Espresso* (online, Sept. 2008); *The Poet's* Haven, no. 6 (online, 2008); *Poetic Matrix* (online letter 6, 2008); and *The Stray Branch* (Spring/Summer 2009).

"Requiem for a Dead Possibility" in *Poetic Hours* (online, UK, Spring 2008); *Flint Hills Review*, Issue 13 (2008); and *The Dirty Napkin* (online, Spring 2009).

"Self-Portrait" in *Wild Violet* (online), Vol. 7, Issue 1; and *Poetic Hours* (online, UK, Spring 2008).

"Shadow in an Anorexic Glass" in *SpeedPoets* (Australia), Vol. 7.4; *Hospital Drive*, Issue 3 (online, Fall 2008); and *CHEST* (online, Mar. 2009).

"Sheltering the Enemy" in *SLANT*, Vol. 4 (Summer 1990); and *Poetry Salzburg Review*, No. 12 (Autumn 2007).

"Sirocco: Wind Song for the Homeless on Market Street" in *Poet's Espresso* (Feb.-Mar. 2009).

"The Ski Slope at Sunset" in *Poet's Ink* (online, Dec. 2008/Jan. 2009); and *Miller's Pond Poetry Magazine* (online, Spring 2009).

"The Song of Popul Vuh" in *Jerry Jazz Musician: Poetry* (online).

"Sins of Omission" in slightly different form in *Literary Mama* (online, Sept. 2007).

"Sonnet for an Unconceived Child" in *Mannequin Envy* (online, Winter 2007); and *Current Accounts*, no. 25 (UK, Winter 2007/8)

"The Spectre of Success" in *Ya'Sou! Ezine* (online, Fall 2008).

"Stairs" in *The Christian Science Monitor* (Home Forum, Nov. 18, 2008).

"A Stranger Called Alzheimer" in *The Reach of Song, Book 7* (1988, Georgia State Poetry Society, Inc.); and *Mannequin Envy* (Winter Melt Issue, Winter/Spring 2009).

"Sunset in Reno" in *Sunken Lines*, no. 6 (online, Autumn 2006); and *The Journal* (once "*of Contemporary Anglo-Scandinavian Poetry*"), no. 17 (Winter 2006/7).

"Survivor" in *San Fernando Poetry Journal*, Vol. 9, No. 3 (1987); and *Ya'Sou! Ezine* (online, Fall 2008).

"Tenting in Lassen Forest" in *Convergence Journal* (online, Winter 2006).

"Terminal Dwelling" in *SpeedPoets* (Australia), Vol. 6.4; *WRITE ON!! Poetry Magazine* (June 2007); *Pulsar*, Edition 2/08 (50) (Sept. 2008); and *nthposition* (online, UK, Feb. 2009).

"Tiara" in *Ascent Aspirations Magazine* (Canada, online, May 2006).

"A Time to Reap" in *Foliate Oak* (online, Sept. 2008); *The Poet's Haven* (online), no. 6; *Poetic Matrix* (online letter 6); and *Pirene's Fountain* (online, Oct. 2008).

"Times of the Year" in *nthposition* (UK, online, Jan. 2007).

"Topography for a Bulimic" in *SpeedPoets* (Australia), Vol. 7.8.

"Tracking the Florida Black Panther" in Jerry Jazz Musician: Poetry (online).

"A Trail to Wounded Knee" in *San Fernando Poetry Journal*, Vol. 9, No. 3 (1987).

"Traveling Beyond Definition" in Poet's Ink (online, May 2008); and SpeedPoets (Australia), Vol. 8.1.

"Twentieth-Century Triptych" in *The Furnace Review* (online, Spring 2008); *The David Jones Society* (Wales, UK, 2009); and *SpeedPoets* (Australia), Vol. 8.2.

"The Velvet Garrote" in *Blue Sky Bodyworks*, no. 11 (1987).

"Victory Song at the Custer Monument" in *Ascent Aspirations Magazine* (Canada, online, Aug. 2008); and *Pulsar*, Edition 2/08 (50) (Sept. 2008).

"Vintage Matrimony" in *The Furnace Review* (online, Spring 2008); *Poetic Hours* (online, UK, Spring 2008); and *Ceremony: a journal of poetry and other arts* (Spring 2009).

"A Vision of Omaha Beach" in *Reach for the Stars* (1986 New Horizons Poetry Anthology); and *Ya'Sou! Ezine* (online, Fall 2008).

"Xmas Eve in Blackjack Town" in *cc&d (Children Churches & Daddies)*, vol. 191 (Dec. 2009); *Bending the Curve*, vol. 191.66 (Oct.-Dec. 2008); and *SpeedPoets* (Australia, 2009).

"The Wheat Fields of Chernobyl" in *Reach for the Stars* (1986 New Horizons Poetry Anthology); *Mannequin Envy* (Winter Melt Issue, Winter/Spring 2009); and *Thick With Conviction* (online, Apr. 2009).

"The Woman Who Walks in the Museum" in *nthposition* (UK, online, Jan. 2007); and *Mannequin Envy* (online, Winter 2007).

"The Writer's Sonnet" in *Chip Off the Writer's Block* (n.d.); and *Poetry Salzburg Review*, No. 14 (Autumn 2008).

"The Writer's Wet Suit" in *The 1986 National Poetry Anthology*, Vol. 6, No. 4 (Winter 1986), ed. John Frost; and *Poetry Salzburg Review*, No. 14 (Autumn 2008).

"The Writer at Half Past Five" in *The Christian Science Monitor* (Home Forum, Oct. 29, 1985).

"Xmas Eve in Blackjack Town," ; and *SpeedPoets* (Australia). Vol. 8.4.

"The Year of Gambler's Anonymous" in *SpeedPoets* (Australia) Vol. 8.5.

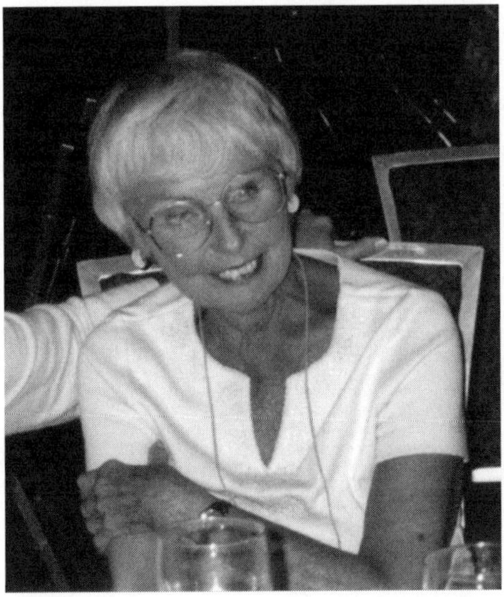

About the Author

A member of the Academy of American Poets, **Suzanne Richardson Harvey** was born in Pittsburgh, Pennsylvania, in 1934. She attended Catholic elementary and secondary schools and later received her B.A. from Mount Mercy College, now Carlow College; an M.A. from Northeastern University, with a thesis on George Meredith; and a Ph.D. from Tufts University, with a specialty in Elizabethan poetry and a dissertation on Edmund Spenser.

After teaching at Tufts, she relocated to the San Francisco Bay Area in Northern California, where for almost two decades she lectured in the English Department at Stanford University. Nearly a decade of her time at Stanford was spent as a resident fellow (together with her husband) in an all-freshmen residence hall. They co-authored a book about this experience entitled *Virtual Reality and the College Freshman: All Our Friends are 18* (Alamo, CA: Alamo Trails Press, 1999).

While at Stanford, she also was a visiting lecturer in the English Department at the University of California at Berkeley. She regularly taught, for nearly a decade, several editorial workshops offered as part of the curriculum for the Publishing Certificate Program at the University of California at Berkeley Extension. Her teaching spawned a book-length manuscript entitled *A Functional Style Manual: Logic and the Art of Writing* that she used as a teaching device in her courses.

She is married, the mother of three adult sons, and the grandmother of five grandsons.